For my publishers Dimitri and Brigitte Sidjanski
and Davy Sidjanski

The Elves
and the Shoemaker

By the Brothers Grimm

RETOLD AND ILLUSTRATED BY

Bernadette Watts

North-South Books

Once upon a time, through sheer bad luck, an honest shoemaker became so poor that he had nothing left in his workshop except enough leather to make a single pair of shoes. Although he was very tired, the good man cut out the shoes and laid the pieces on the workbench ready to sew them the next day. Then he went to bed and slept peacefully.

The next morning the shoemaker went into his workshop
and there, to his great surprise, he saw a finished pair of shoes!

He looked at the shoes carefully. He examined the soles and the uppers, but he could not find one careless stitch. They were perfect!

Early that day a customer came along. The shoes delighted him and were exactly what he needed. In fact, he was so pleased he paid a very good price.

With this money the shoemaker bought fresh food for himself and his family, and enough fine leather to make two more pairs of shoes.

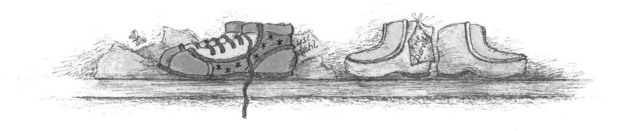

That evening, with renewed energy, the shoemaker cut out the leather shapes for two pairs of shoes. Then, feeling content, he went to bed.

The shoemaker rose early the next morning to start work, but there was no need! For there on the workbench were two pairs of shoes, as beautifully sewn as the first.

Customers soon came along and paid good prices for the shoes. Then the shoemaker bought enough leather for four more pairs.

Overnight the four pairs were made. And so it went on. Whatever he cut out in the evening was finished the next morning. Soon he was a wealthy man again.

After finishing work one evening, just before Christmas, the shoemaker said to his wife: "Shall we stay up tonight, to find out who has been helping us?"

His wife liked the idea. So they lit a candle, hid behind some clothes which were hanging on pegs, and kept watch.

At midnight, two little naked men came in. They jumped onto the workbench, gathered up the cut-out leather and then began to stitch and sew and hammer with such skill and speed the shoemaker was amazed. The little men worked hard without stopping. When the shoes were completely finished they hurried away.

The next morning the shoemaker's wife said: "The little men have made us rich, and we really must show our gratitude. They must be so cold, running about without a stitch of clothes to wear. I have an idea! I will make them each a shirt, a

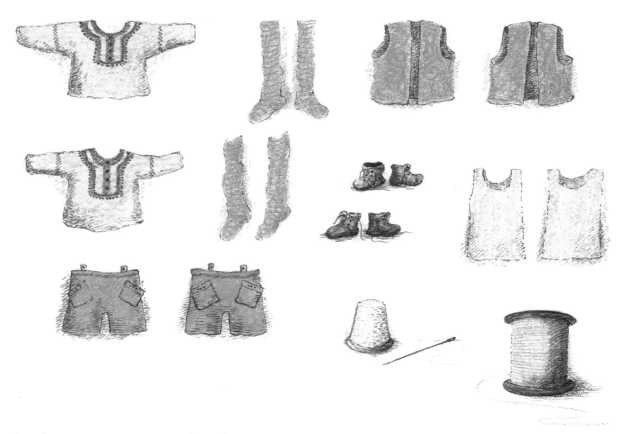

jacket, a vest, a pair of trousers, and I'll knit them each a pair of warm stockings. And you can make them each a pair of fine shoes."

"That's an excellent plan!" agreed the shoemaker. So, on Christmas Eve, instead of laying out the leather they arranged their gifts on the table. Then they hid and waited for the little men to arrive.

At midnight the little men came bounding in, eager to get to work. But they found no leather, only the pretty little clothes and shoes. At first they were puzzled. Then they were delighted! They dressed quickly and then they jumped around and sang:

"Now we are boys so fine to see,
Why should we longer cobblers be!"

They danced and skipped around the room. Finally they danced out the door and disappeared.

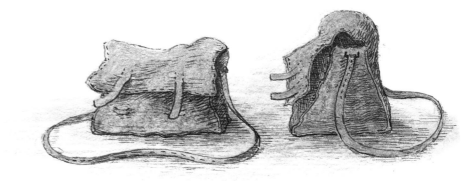

The little men never returned. But as long as the shoemaker lived, everything went well for him and all his efforts were rewarded.